Unraveling Mr. Ashford

A Flirty, Spicy Romcom with a Grumpy Tech Billionaire, a Sunshine Chaos Bomb, and a Storm That Changed Everything

Hana York

Pink Pop Publishing

Unraveling Mr. Ashford

(Don't Fall for the Billionaire Book 3)

Copyright © 2025 by Hana York

www.HanaYork.com

Contents

1. Chapter One   1

2. Chapter Two   9

3. Chapter Three   16

4. Chapter Four   24

5. Chapter Five   34

6. Chapter Six   43

7. Chapter Seven   53

8. Chapter Eight   61

9. Chapter Nine   70

10. Epilogue   76

11. Hana York Books   85

12. About the Author   87

Chapter One

MIA

I WAS ABOUT TO land in paradise—and if I kept grinning like the Chesire Cat, I might actually prove my mom right: my face *could* get stuck that way. But who cared? After the Great Vision Board Inferno of last week—yes, it *literally* caught fire—I'd taken it as a sign. I was overdue for a break.

So I called Liz. Who called Brett. Who called Logan.

And now? I was on a boat headed to a private island, courtesy of the world's most well-connected favor chain. Just me, Mia Wilder—overcaffeinated chaos goddess—on my way to a man-made oasis where the only thing on my agenda was doing absolutely nothing.

"Alright, universe," I said, arms wide to the sea breeze, "hit me with your best vacation vibes. I'm ready."

The boatman glanced at me like he was debating whether to offer a lifejacket for enthusiasm-induced overboard risks. But I didn't care. This was my time. No dead-lines. No emails. Just me, the ocean, and whatever cocktail came with a paper umbrella and questionable fruit garnish.

As we neared the island, the tension I hadn't even realized I was holding began to unravel. Each tiny island had its own bungalow, tucked into palm trees like something off a movie poster. Quiet. Secluded. Bliss.

The second we bumped the dock, I was on my feet—bag slung over one shoulder, hat in hand, ready to disembark.

"Thanks for the ride!" I called as I stepped onto the dock, giving the boatman a wave he didn't return. Rude. But whatever. I was unreachable now. Possibly glowing. Definitely smug.

I paused for a slow, dramatic spin. Theme music: internal. Vibe: tropical main character energy.

The bungalow sat nestled between swaying palms and completely unfair postcard-level views. There was even a hammock. A *hammock*. I had arrived.

The air smelled like sea salt, warm breeze, and pure freedom. I followed the winding stone path up to the front door, trailing my fingers across the fronds like I was starring in a spa commercial. No people. No notifications. No inbox from hell. Just me and whatever was waiting inside.

The door swung open into a space that was bright, breezy, and gave off serious *rich people Pinterest board* energy. Fruit on the counter. Towels rolled with spiritual intent. A bar cart.

It was perfect.

"This is it," I whispered, pausing in the doorway like I was about to marry the space. "We're in love. I live here now. Someone forward my mail."

I tossed my bag onto the couch with dramatic flair—because if you weren't making a grand entrance for an audience of throw pillows, were you even vacationing properly?

Step one: unpack essentials. Sunglasses. SPF 50. Journal. Three pens. Emergency chocolate. Backup emergency chocolate. Sketchbook I swore I wouldn't touch. Not even once.

I stared at it for a beat, the blank cover practically whispering *you know you want to*. "Nope," I muttered, tossing it face-down on the coffee table like it couldn't seduce me if I avoided eye contact. "You are not the boss of me."

Next stop: the bedroom.

It had a four-poster bed draped in gauzy white curtains and approximately fifty-seven pillows. The kind of setup that whispered *you are adored, and your spine will be perfectly aligned by morning*. I flopped onto the mattress with a happy sigh and immediately did a snow angel—luxury linen edition.

"This is fine," I told the ceiling. "This is totally normal."

Back in the main room, I cracked open the mini-fridge and gasped. Sparkling water. Fresh juice. Chocolate-covered almonds. And one of those tiny glass bottles of milk like you'd find at a farmer's market curated by influencers with goats.

Juice in hand, I stepped outside.

The deck had a private plunge pool and two lounge chairs angled like they were in a competition for best ocean view. I sank into one like a queen returning to her throne—juice in one hand, sunglasses perched like a crown, hair already frizzing in joyful rebellion. Whatever. I was relaxed. I was glowing. I was *totally* not wondering if my sketchbook missed me.

I closed my eyes and soaked it in—the breeze, the waves, the beautiful absence of anyone needing anything from me.

This was the right choice.

Definitely the right—

CRACK.

My eyes flew open.

Was that thunder?

I glanced at the horizon.

The sky, which had been a soft watercolor of vacation bliss, now had a dramatic smear of gray creeping in from the edge. One cloud. Maybe two. But definitely not enough to panic over.

"Do not ruin this for me," I whispered at the ocean, pointing my juice like a tiny, citrus-scented threat.

GRANT

The boat rocked harder than expected as we crossed the last stretch of open water. I stayed seated, jaw tight, one hand gripping the edge of the bench—not because I was nervous. Just tired. The kind of tired that sleep didn't fix. The kind you carried in your bones after too many meetings, too many "urgent" emails, too many people who saw a title, not a person.

The boatman glanced back. "You sure about this? Storm's rolling in faster than expected."

I exhaled through my nose. "I'll be fine."

He checked again a minute later. "If it hits hard, you might lose signal for a while."

"Perfect," I muttered. "I didn't come to talk to anyone."

He gave me a look—half annoyed, half curious—but left it alone.

Good. I wasn't here to explain myself. I came to disappear. To shut the world out for a while. If a little weather helped keep it at bay? Even better.

By the time we reached the dock, the clouds had thickened, the sky gone from pale blue to a heavy slate gray. Wind pushed against the hull, rough enough to knock the boat harder than it should've against the dock.

I slung my duffel over my shoulder and stepped off without waiting for help.

"Last chance," the boatman said, still eyeing the horizon. "Sure you don't want to ride it out at the main resort?"

"This is the plan," I said. "I'll be fine."

He didn't argue. Just nodded and shifted into reverse. Within seconds, the hum of the engine was swallowed by wind and waves.

I stood there a beat longer, watching him disappear. The bungalow sat tucked between the palms, quiet and pristine. Everything I'd asked for.

Everything I needed.

I just hoped the storm—whatever kind it turned out to be—held off long enough to let me breathe.

The path to the bungalow wound through swaying trees, damp fronds brushing my shoulders, the scent of rain already in the air. A few coconuts dotted the trail like nature's speed bumps. The wind picked up, first drops of rain tapping the roof as I stepped onto the porch.

From the outside, it looked exactly like I'd hoped.

Quiet. Still.

Then I opened the door—and flinched.

Music.

Loud, bright, aggressively cheerful music blasted through the space like it was prepping for a bachelorette weekend. And there—spinning barefoot in the center of the room—was a woman.

Pink bikini top. Sarong slipping off one hip. Hair wild and curly, bouncing with every step. Lips moving along with the lyrics like she was the star of her own music video. Effortless. Radiant.

Beautiful.

The kind of beautiful that made you pause. That made it hard not to notice the smooth legs, the swing of her hips, the soft glow of her skin.

And my body—utter traitor—noticed all of it.

I told myself to look away.

I didn't.

Instead, I stood there. Stunned. Irritated. A little alarmed at how fast my brain forgot why I came here in the first place.

This was not part of the plan.

I came for silence.

Not a barefoot sun goddess twirling through my sanctuary like she *was* the weather.

I cleared my throat.

Loudly.

She didn't hear me.

Of course she didn't.

So I stepped fully inside, letting the door slam shut behind me.

She shrieked and skidded to a stop, nearly slipping on her own sarong, eyes going wide like I'd materialized out of thin air.

"WHAT THE ACTUAL HELL—WHO ARE YOU?! Are you lost? Are you a serial killer? Because I've got to tell you, *today is not the day!*"

"I could ask you the same thing," I said, deadpan. "This is supposed to be *my* bungalow."

And just like that, peace was officially off the itinerary.

Chapter Two

MIA

HE WAS GRUMPY.

And tall.

And did I mention grumpy?

What in the brooding, broad-shouldered lumberjack fantasy had just walked through my door?

I blinked, still holding my juice like a weapon, trying to process the fact that the human embodiment of a moody Greek god was standing in my sacred, self-care sanctuary looking like I'd personally offended him by existing.

"This is supposed to be your bungalow?" I repeated, breathless. "Oh no. Nope. Absolutely not."

He didn't answer—just stood there, jaw tight, arms crossed, silently judging me and possibly all spontaneous dance breaks.

But his eyes were kind. Unfairly so. The kind that said he'd help old ladies cross the street without waiting for thanks. And those shoulders? They could absolutely carry a roof beam. Or me. Through a flood. Probably shirtless.

Focus, Mia.

"Yes, my bungalow," he said, dragging a hand through his hair like I'd just asked him to solve a Rubik's cube in the dark. "Booked through the week."

"You're joking."

He was not joking. He looked like he didn't know how to joke.

Muscles. Mood. Mystery. And now: a walking, talking cancellation of my spa-vibes-only vacation plan.

This was supposed to be *my* week. Hammocks. Face masks. Utter, uninterrupted bliss.

Not... this.

Definitely not *him*.

I grabbed the phone and stabbed in the resort number like I was starting a duel. "We'll see about this, Mr. Tall-Dark-and-Uninvited," I muttered. "You may be hot, but you're also extremely grumpy, which cancels out, like, sixty percent of the appeal."

A low voice behind me: "Did you just call me hot?"

I jumped. "No. I mean—yes. But not in a *come hither* way. More like an observational data point. Like 'the sky is blue' or 'fruit should not be room temperature'."

He just stared at me. Unmoved. Like I'd said I was building a shrine to throw pillows and anxiety.

"And anyway," I added, flailing for dignity, "it doesn't count if you're *that* grumpy."

Still nothing.

Tall. Judgy. Unbothered. Gorgeous.

"Okay, seriously," I muttered, turning away. "Stop looking at me like that. I'm flustered, not unhinged. Just... unhinged-adjacent."

The line picked up. A cheerful voice chirped, "Hi, Isla Cove Resort—how can I—"

"Yes! Hi! " I said, too loud and too fast. "There's been a mistake. I'm on Island Seven, and there's a man here. Like, a full-grown *grumpy* man. Not a staff member. Not a hallucination. Real. Broody. Cheekbones that could start wars—anyway, not important."

Grant crossed his arms tighter. Statue mode: activated.

"I was told this bungalow was mine for the week," I pressed on. "But apparently Mr. 'Resting Glare Face' got the same memo. So if someone could just—"

Crack.

A pop. Then static. Then nothing.

I stared at the phone. "No, no, no. Don't you die on me now, signal bar. You were my last hope."

Dead. Gone. Zero bars.

I lifted the phone like a peace offering to the sky. "Come on," I hissed. "Not when I've just declared war on a man who bench-presses silence for sport."

The man didn't say a word. But I felt his stare.

I turned my back to him and moved toward the window, waving the phone like I was summoning a miracle. No signal. No help. No justice.

"Okay," I whispered. "Not panicking. This is fine. I'm not stranded on a private island with a hot stranger who thinks I'm in *his* bungalow."

And then—because of course—the skies opened up.

Buckets of rain. Wind howling. Palms bent sideways. A pair of flip-flops launched off the porch like they were trying to escape the narrative.

When I turned around, *he* was still standing there. Annoyed. A little smug.

"Looks like we're both stuck," I said flatly.

GRANT

The rain slammed against the roof like it had a vendetta.

I pulled out my phone, already knowing what I'd see. One bar. Then none.

"No signal," I muttered.

Across the room, the woman I was apparently stranded with let out a dramatic sigh and dropped onto the couch like the storm had personally betrayed her.

"Spectacular," she muttered. "Just absolutely peak timing. Stuck on an island with Mr. Corporate Brood and zero internet. This is fine. Totally fine. Like, aggressively fine."

I didn't respond.

Partly because I didn't trust myself not to laugh. Mostly because I still wasn't convinced this wasn't some kind of cosmic prank.

She waved her juice glass toward me without looking. "Okay. Since we're doing this, I need to vet you."

"Vet me?"

"Yes. I've seen this movie. Guy shows up during a storm, no one can verify his identity, and boom—surprise murder."

"I'm not a murderer," I said flatly.

She squinted. "That's exactly what a murderer would say."

I exhaled slowly. "What do you want to know?"

"Name. Job. Zodiac sign. Go."

I gave her a look, but she just raised her brows like she was taking attendance.

"Grant Ashford. CEO. Virgo."

Her eyes narrowed slightly. "Virgo. Yeah, that explains the vibe."

I had no idea what that meant, and I wasn't about to ask.

She leaned forward, studying me like a case study. "CEO of what?"

"Tech. Infrastructure. Startups. Boring stuff."

She whistled. "So you're rich-rich."

"I'm tired-tired."

That seemed to catch her off guard. Her smirk faltered for a beat.

"Okay. Noted. Broody, maybe-human tech guy. Virgo. Probably sleeps in spreadsheets."

I arched a brow. "And you? Or do I just assume the barefoot Bond girl twirling through my living room isn't the real threat here?"

Her face lit up like I'd handed her a trophy. "Did you just call me a Bond girl?"

"I meant assassin."

She waved a hand. "Still counts."

Of course it did.

She stood, struck a pose, and gestured like cameras were rolling. "Mia Wilder. Product designer. Sagittarius. Chaos in a cute wrapper. Also? Not a serial killer. Recovering perfectionist with a caffeine dependency and a tendency to monologue under pressure."

I blinked.

She grinned. "And no, I'm not always like this. Sometimes I'm worse."

I looked at her. At the sarong. The wild hair. The hurricane energy wrapped in sun-kissed skin.

Then I reached for a chair.

Because apparently, I was going to need to sit down.

Chapter Three

MIA

HE SAT DOWN LIKE my entire personality physically exhausted him.

Which—rude.

I mean, I'd just delivered a deluxe introduction: charm, facts, sparkle rating solidly nine out of ten. The least he could do was pretend to be impressed instead of staring at me like I was a walking migraine in a pink sarong.

Classic grump.

He sat. I hovered. Not because I was nervous—please—I *thrive* in chaos. I just needed a minute to recalibrate. To mentally map out how one survives being stranded with a hot, emotionally constipated tech billionaire whose idea of vulnerability is switching to decaf.

"So," I said, hands on hips. "Ground rules."

Grant Ashford looked up like I'd suggested a corporate trust fall.

"Rules," he repeated flatly.

"Yes. We're two strangers stuck on an island in a storm. One bungalow. One bed. High potential for emotional implosion. We need parameters."

He just stared at me.

"Sleeping arrangements," I added. "You get the couch. Obviously."

His brow lifted. Dangerously slow. "Why is that obvious?"

"I was here first. And I already flopped on the bed, which makes it mine by squatter's rights."

He pinched the bridge of his nose like I'd caused him physical pain."Fine. You get the bed."

"Thank you." I gave him a gracious nod. "Next: bathroom etiquette. Closed door means knock. Open door also means knock. Touch my skincare, and I'll hex you."

Flat stare. "I brought my own."

"Well," I said, flopping into the armchair, "look at Mr. Self-Sufficient. I can tell we're going to be best friends."

He didn't respond. Just leaned back with his arms crossed like he was silently calculating how long he could survive before the storm—or I—broke him.

I squinted at him. Not threateningly—scientifically.

He looked like someone who color-coded his inbox and ironed his socks. Under all that broody control-freak energy? Annoyingly, objectively hot.

"You know," I said, tilting my head, "you give off serious 'my calendar is optimized for maximum efficiency' vibes."

Nothing.

"Do you have a spreadsheet for emotional regulation? A pie chart for trust issues?"

Still nothing. Was he rebooting?

I waved a hand. "Hello? Earth to Grant. I'm trying to bond here."

He sighed—long, suffering, the kind you save for dental appointments and DMV lines.

"Right," I muttered. "Best friends it is."

I stood. I needed a break. From the silence. From the tension. From the way he looked at me like I was a pop-up ad he couldn't close.

"I'm going to assess the storm," I declared. "You stay here and continue brooding into the furniture."

He stood too—probably to argue—but thought better of it.

I marched to the door, flung it open like I was personally in charge of the weather—and got slammed in the face with wind.

The wind howled, and my hair whipped around like it was auditioning for a shampoo commercial. My sarong took flight. And a second later, it smacked into Grant like some sort of pastel heat-seeking missile. It hit him square in the chest, wrapped once around his shoulder like a very confused fashion statement, and just… stayed there.

He didn't move. Just stared down at the fabric clinging to his chest.

Then—very slowly—he lifted his eyes to me.

"Was this part of the rules?" he asked, deadpan. "Or are we improvising now?"

"ARE YOU KIDDING ME?" I shrieked, slamming the door and pointing at him like he'd just committed a felony.

He looked down at the fabric stuck to him. One brow arched.

"You lost something," he said.

"I KNOW," I snapped. "I was *wearing* that!"

His gaze dragged down my now-sarongless body, lingering just long enough to make my skin buzz.

"So I noticed," he said calmly. "Hard not to."

I made a strangled sound, lunged forward, and yanked the sarong from his shoulder like it had betrayed me.

"I hate everything," I muttered, rewrapping it with the grace of someone losing a fight with humidity and pride.

He didn't laugh.

But the look on his face?

That smug, not-quite-smile?

Absolutely weaponized.

GRANT

I wasn't proud of it, but I forgot how to speak for a second.

She shrieked, snatched the sarong like it had committed a felony, and rewrapped herself with all the flustered dignity of a woman wronged by the weather.

And I just stood there. Frozen. Not laughing. But God help me—I wanted to.

The glare. The blush. The way her hands fumbled with fabric like it owed her an apology.

Ridiculous.

And... stunning.

Not the kind of polished, posed beauty I saw at charity galas and launch events. No, Mia was barefoot chaos. Sun-kissed skin, windblown curls, and a spark in her eyes that dared the world to keep up. A woman designed by nature to dismantle structure.

I turned to the kitchen. I needed cold. I needed order. I needed the fridge.

I opened it like it might give me clarity and stared at an overly curated lineup of juices, herbs, and artisanal bottled water.

None of it helped.

Across the room, she was muttering to herself while re-arranging the welcome fruit like it had personally wronged her.

"Papaya," she said, nudging it like a grudge. "Statement fruit. Nobody eats it unless they're trying to prove something."

She adjusted a banana. Eyed the pineapple like it had spoken out of turn.

"Too much citrus in one corner. Amateur move. Basic fruit feng shui."

I stared out the window, trying to out-storm the storm. Rain blurred the view. Wind howled like it was insulted. The palm trees bent at angles that seemed medically un-wise.

Still no help.

Then, blessedly, silence.

"What are you doing?" she asked behind me.

"Reevaluating my definition of 'vacation,'" I muttered.

She made a noise—somewhere between a laugh and a groan. "Great. So. What's for dinner?"

I blinked, looked over my shoulder. She was perched on the couch's arm like a gremlin in vacation mode, eyebrows lifted like she expected an actual answer.

"You think I'm cooking?"

"I'm not," she said brightly. "I'm in vacation mode. I don't cook in vacation mode."

"Do you cook out of vacation mode?"

"Not if I can help it."

I sighed and reopened the fridge with the resignation of a man preparing to wage war against a gourmet grocery haul.

"Wagyu filet. Truffle butter. Three kinds of heirloom carrots. Who the hell stocks this stuff?"

She let out a delighted gasp. "This fridge is fancier than my last relationship."

I didn't turn. "That's a low bar."

"Excuse you. It was a very decorative relationship. Zero substance. High aesthetic."

I almost smiled.

Almost.

Still staring into the fridge, I said, "At least we won't starve."

"You're doing great," she chirped.

I turned. "You could help."

"I *am* helping. With morale. I'm the vibe manager."

I handed her a cutting board. She blinked at it.

"I don't chop," she said. "I curate."

"Then curate the carrots. By height, color, emotional baggage. Dealer's choice."

She grinned. "Height and mood. Obviously."

And somehow, we were cooking together.

Quiet. Almost comfortable.

The knives tapped gently against the counter. Outside, the storm kept roaring, but in here—it was calm. As calm as it could be with Mia narrating the emotional backstory of every herb.

I'd cooked with people before—on dates, at events, while making polite conversation. But this? This felt different.

Close.

Familiar in a way that had no right to feel familiar.

Her shoulder brushed mine. Her laugh skimmed over my skin. I caught myself watching her hands instead of the knife.

I turned my focus to the steak.

Because I didn't come here for this.

And I really wasn't ready for how easy she made it feel.

Chapter Four

Mia

"This is delicious," I declared, closing my eyes like I was on a cooking show. "Perfect sear. Subtle seasoning. A delicate whisper of truffle. Honestly, I should be on the Food Network by now."

Grant looked at me over his wine glass. "You cut two carrots."

"And arranged them artfully," I said, gesturing to the plates like I was unveiling a museum exhibit. "Plating is half the experience."

He didn't argue—just returned to his steak like being casually excellent was his default setting.

I stabbed a carrot, chewed thoughtfully, then pointed my fork at him. "So, Mr. Broody Tech Billionaire Virgo, why are you here?"

He glanced at the window, where the wind whipped the palm trees like it had a vendetta. "Storm. Wrong bungalow. Trapped by weather. General chaos."

I rolled my eyes. "Not physically here. I mean why *here* here—this island. No people. No Wi-Fi. No DoorDash."

He set down his knife, took a sip of wine, and stared at the table like weighing his answer against the likelihood I'd make another papaya joke.

Finally, he said, "I needed quiet."

"From what?"

A beat. Then: "Everything. My company. My calendar. The constant noise of being needed."

I nodded, chewing slower. "So you came to detox from humanity."

He looked at me, meeting my eyes for real this time. "Basically."

"And then you got me," I said with a grin.

That earned the tiniest twitch at the corner of his mouth. "Basically."

I leaned forward, fork still in hand. "So let me get this straight—you came out here for monk-level solitude... and instead got a surprise plus-one who talks too much, claims half the bungalow by force of personality, and has zero respect for your existential brooding?"

He arched a brow. "That's one way to put it."

"I'm an acquired taste," I said, swirling my wine. "Like olives. Or socks with sandals. Once you're in, though—very on trend."

He shook his head, but the almost-smile was still there.

"Ironically," I added, "I came here for the same reason."

His brows lifted. "You?"

"Shocking, I know. But yes. I, Mia Wilder—chaotic, caffeinated, allegedly allergic to stillness—needed quiet, too."

I tapped my fingers against my glass. "I was tired of always doing, fixing, being everything for everyone. I wanted stillness. A hammock. A hard reset."

He didn't speak at first. Just watched me with something softer in his eyes. Something that made me feel... understood.

"Guess we picked the wrong island," he said.

"Or," I nudged his foot lightly under the table, "the universe picked the right one. We just haven't figured out why yet."

He didn't pull away. But he didn't answer either.

The silence stretched, but it felt full. Not awkward. Like a story waiting to begin.

We stood together, wine warm in our cheeks. I reached for my plate just as he reached for his, our hands brushing.

Just a spark.

Nothing major.

Definitely nothing I'd overanalyze later. Probably.

"Thanks for cooking," I said. "And for not insulting my expert carrot placement."

"I didn't say I wasn't judging," he said, voice low, amused.

I made it halfway to the sink before it happened.

BOOM.

Thunder cracked, sharp and loud. The windows rattled. The lights flickered.

And just like that—pitch black.

I screamed.

Not dramatically.

Okay, dramatically.

Before realizing what I was doing, I'd launched myself across the kitchen like a flying squirrel and *latched* onto Grant.

"JESUS, TAKE THE WHEEL," I shrieked, full koala mode, arms and legs wrapped around him like he was the last tree in a lightning storm.

He didn't fall.

Didn't stumble.

Just... stood there. Solid. Warm. Unreasonably calm.

"Darkness," I gasped against his neck. "Unnatural. Terrifying. Betrayal by electricity."

His hands were hovering like he didn't quite know what to do with me. "Are you—are you afraid of the dark?"

"No," I said, clearly lying. "I'm afraid of—uh—*surprise ambiance.*"

He made a low, strangled sound that might have been a laugh. "You jumped on me like I was a life raft."

"Don't flatter yourself," I muttered, not moving. "You're tall and sturdy. This is purely survival instinct."

Grant shifted slightly, and I realized I was still clinging to him like a wind-chime in a hurricane.

"I'm going to set you down now," he said, voice dry.

"Fine," I huffed, loosening my grip. "But if something jumps out of the shadows, I'm climbing back up."

GRANT

One second, I was clearing the table.

The next, she was wrapped around me like I'd just pulled her from a burning building—arms around my neck, legs around my waist, face pressed against my throat. A human exclamation point who smelled like coconut and chaos.

And my body?

Fully betraying me.

A bolt of heat shot through me, and my hands—traitorous—found her hips. Steadying her. Anchoring her. Not because I meant to. Just because she was there, and I was a man, and she was—

God.

Soft. Warm. Maddening. From her frantic breathing to the way she muttered like the storm owed her money.

I'd come here for peace. Stillness.

Not this.

But here she was, clinging to me like I was the only thing keeping her grounded. And my body responded like it had been waiting for her all along.

Unacceptable. Unsettling. Unavoidable.

"I'm going to set you down now," I said, my voice rougher than I intended.

She huffed something vaguely threatening and loosened her grip. I set her down, hands lingering longer than they should've.

The moment she stepped back, the air felt colder.

She crossed her arms. "That wasn't a scream, by the way. It was a—battle cry."

"Of course it was," I muttered, turning to grab the emergency candles before I started thinking about how good she'd felt in my arms.

The match flared. Light hit her face—wide-eyed, flushed, lips parted like she still hadn't caught her breath.

Neither had I.

The match burned too close. I swore softly and shook it out.

Lit another. Soft glow. Long shadows. The bungalow looked different like this. Quieter. Intimate. Like it was holding its breath.

So was I.

She watched me pretending not to. When I handed her a candle, she raised a brow. "So this is what we're working with?"

"Seems like it."

She nodded. "Not the worst lighting I've seen."

"Glad it meets your standards."

I moved into the living room. She followed, her bare feet whispering across the floor.

The silence returned—but it wasn't peaceful. It was the kind that made everything louder in my head.

The soft rustle of her steps. The way her hair caught the candlelight. That barely-there smile she didn't know she was wearing.

"Okay," she said, slicing through the silence. "We're officially one thunderclap away from romantic horror movie territory. Love that for us."

I huffed a laugh and lit the last candle.

She was close.

Too close.

And I didn't move.

Neither did she.

She studied me like she couldn't decide if I was fascinating or infuriating. Odds were even.

The candlelight softened everything—edges, shadows, restraint.

Bad idea.

"You okay?" she asked.

I nodded. Too tight. The kind of nod you give when you're lying to everyone, including yourself.

"You sure?" she pressed, voice low. "You look like you're either solving a math problem or plotting an escape."

"Little of both," I muttered.

She laughed.

Not polite. Not forced.

Real. Warm.

And just like that, I was wrecked.

The feeling hit low and hard, curling through me like something I'd been avoiding for years.

I stepped back. Useless.

"We should probably call it a night," I said, keeping my voice neutral. "Long travel day. Hopefully the storm clears and we can figure out whatever booking glitch landed us in the same GPS coordinates."

She nodded. "Sleep. Great idea." Then perked up. "Bathroom first?"

I gestured toward the hall. "Be my guest."

She lifted her candle like she was leading a séance and swept off with dramatic solemnity. "If I'm not back in ten minutes, assume the storm swallowed me whole."

"If you disappear, I'm claiming the bed," I called after her.

Ten minutes later, she returned—hair in a bun, skin shiny from whatever ritual had just taken place.

"Your turn," she said, handing over the candle like it was sacred.

The bathroom smelled like coconut and something botanical I didn't want to think about too hard.

When I came back, she was frowning at the candles.

"We probably shouldn't leave these burning," she said. "Unless you want to wake up in a luxury bonfire."

Fair.

I snuffed them out one by one. The room dimmed with every puff.

"I left you a blanket and pillow," she added, already retreating toward the bedroom. "No booby traps."

"Appreciated."

"Oh—and I get the bathroom first in the morning."

"Noted."

She paused in the doorway, glanced back. "Night, Grant."

"Night, Mia."

The door clicked shut.

And then it was just me. The dark. The storm.

And the lingering scent of coconut.

Chapter Five

MIA

I WAS FINE.

Totally, absolutely, one hundred percent fine.

Just a woman in a luxury bungalow, curled up in a bed the size of a small country, trying not to flinch every time the storm tested the structural integrity of the roof.

Fine.

Lightning flashed. Thunder cracked loud enough to shake the windows. My pulse sprinted.

"Okay," I whispered to the ceiling, "maybe not fine-fine. More like... functional fine."

I yanked the blanket up to my chin.

The wind shrieked. Something thudded. Something else creaked. I squeaked.

This was ridiculous. I was Mia Wilder—independent, overcaffeinated, chaos-certified—but I'd survived worse.

Corporate meltdowns. Artistic burnout. That tequila-fueled birthday in Cabo.

Surely I could handle a little atmospheric drama.

Unless the dark came with ghost noises and judgmental bungalow groans.

I flipped over. Then back. Then again.

Blanket off. Blanket on. Blanket off.

I glared at the ceiling. "This is fine. This is totally, completely—"

BOOM.

That one shook the bed.

I sat up, hair sticking out like an electrocuted hedgehog.

Absolutely not. No way. I was not asking him. I would sooner hold a séance to summon my own emotional support ghost.

I threw off the covers.

Thirty seconds later, I padded down the hallway in my oversized sleep shirt, bun a mess, holding a candle like I was about to summon spirits.

I paused at the edge of the living room.

Grant lay stretched out on the couch—bare chest, broad shoulders, and all six feet of broody logic in one deeply inconvenient package.

This was a mistake.

I was not doing this.

Except I totally was.

I cleared my throat.

He shifted but didn't open his eyes. "You good?"

"Define good."

One eye cracked open. He blinked, then slowly sat up. "What's wrong?"

I clutched the candle tighter. "Okay. So. Hypothetically... if someone—me—were slightly, mildly, extremely freaked out by the darkness and the horror movie happening outside... would it be the worst thing if that someone asked you to maybe sleep in the same room?"

Silence.

"I mean, it's a huge bed," I added quickly. "We'd have our own zip codes. I wouldn't even notice unless you started snoring in binary."

Still nothing.

"Or not," I backpedaled. "Totally fine. I can go back. Curl up with the throw pillows and my crushing sense of shame. That works too."

Another crack of thunder.

Grant stood.

No words. No grumbling. Not even a sigh.

He just grabbed his pillow and walked past me—silent, solid, and unfairly steady as the wind howled like a banshee behind us.

I followed like a guilty toddler.

Inside the bedroom, the candle cast long shadows. He paused at the foot of the bed like he was doing spatial calculations.

"This thing's massive," he muttered.

"Right?" I whispered, like the bed might be flattered. "Enough space for three awkward coworkers and a life coach."

He shook his head and walked around to the far side.

I scrambled to mine, threw myself under the covers, and tried to act casual.

Totally chill. Not at all aware that the hot, emotionally reserved tech guy was now adjusting a pillow on the same mattress.

Still shirtless, he lay back with a long exhale.

Neither of us spoke. The candle flickered on the nightstand. The storm growled outside.

The air felt... still.

"Thanks," I whispered.

"For what?"

"For not laughing. Or calling me ridiculous. Or ignoring me completely."

A pause. Then, "You're not ridiculous."

"Wow," I said. "Compliment accepted. Writing that in my mental scrapbook."

Another pause.

"You're just... loud."

I snorted into the pillow. "And you're emotionally constipated."

He didn't deny it.

Thunder rolled again.

But this time, I didn't flinch.

Maybe because he was here.

Maybe because he didn't feel like the kind of guy who'd let the storm get in.

"I don't snore," he said suddenly.

I turned my head. "What?"

"You said something about binary snoring."

"Oh. Right." I smiled. "Good to know."

A beat.

"Do you?"

"Snore?" I lifted a brow. "Only if I've had dairy. Or spent the day suppressing emotional turmoil."

"So... yes."

I grinned into the dark. "Goodnight, Grant."

He was quiet for a second.

Then: "Goodnight, Mia."

GRANT

This wasn't how I pictured the week going.

I came for silence. For space. For a break from being the guy who fixed everything.

Instead, I got her.

Mia Wilder—curled up on the opposite side of the bed like it was hers by right. One foot kicked out from beneath the covers. Her hair was a halo of chaos across the pillow. Breathing even. Shoulders finally relaxed.

Not asleep. Not yet. But close.

The storm still roared outside, but she wasn't flinching anymore.

Because I was here.

And that shouldn't have made something tighten in my chest.

I turned onto my back and stared at the ceiling. The battery-powered candle I'd found glowed on the nightstand, casting soft shadows and too much clarity.

I could see her.

The curve of her shoulder. The freckle near her collarbone. Her parted lips, her quiet breath. I could still feel her clinging to me earlier—legs, arms, voice in my ear like I was the only solid thing in a storm.

It wasn't just that she was beautiful—though, God, she was. It was the way she existed. Loud. Unfiltered. Fearless.

Like the world was hers to narrate and bend into something brighter.

She was chaos.

And I did not do chaos.

I did order. Discipline. Control. That's how I built everything that mattered.

So why the hell was I lying next to a human supernova, wide awake, and not thinking about any of that?

I closed my eyes. I wasn't going to touch her. Wasn't going to move. I'd sleep. Wait out the storm.

That was the plan.

But it wasn't just physical anymore.

It was her laugh in the kitchen. Her battle cries over fruit. The way she made me forget about deadlines and deliverables and the gnawing ache of never being enough.

I must've drifted off somewhere between denial and resignation.

And then—

I was dreaming.

Sunlight filtered through open doors. A breeze carried the scent of citrus and salt. Mia danced barefoot in the kitchen, wearing an oversized white button-down that barely hit mid-thigh. Her hair was a mess. Her smile was not.

She twirled around the floor like it was a stage, claiming the room with narration I didn't understand but never wanted to stop hearing.

And then she was walking toward me.

Slow. Intentional.

Her eyes locked on mine—challenging, curious, unafraid.

She reached up, fingers brushing my collarbone, pausing there.

"I think the universe knew what it was doing," she whispered.

Then her mouth touched mine.

Soft. Testing.

And I broke.

I kissed her like she was the only thing tethering me to earth. Like I'd been waiting for this without knowing it. Her hands slid under my shirt. Mine found her waist, her back, the shape of her.

"Grant," she gasped—and it undid me.

I lifted her, carried her to the bed, laid her down like she was holy.

She looked up at me, laughing, wild, radiant.

I leaned in.

CRACK.

Thunder split the sky.

I jolted awake, heart pounding.

The candle still glowed. The storm still screamed. And Mia was still beside me, turned away, blanket curled tight.

The dream was gone.

But the feeling?

That stayed.

It wasn't just the kiss I didn't want to lose. It was what came with it—the wake-up call. The pull. The terrifying, magnetic realization that something in me had shifted.

And she was the reason.

I wasn't sleeping again. Not now. Not with her so close and the storm still howling—outside, and in me.

Quietly, I slid out of bed and headed for the living room.

Chapter Six

MIA

I WOKE UP WARM.

Which, considering the storm still sounded like it was auditioning for the apocalypse, was unexpected.

The bed was soft. The blanket cocoon-level cozy. For one blissful second, I just floated—half-asleep, half-aware.

Then I noticed it.

Something was missing.

Someone.

I opened one eye, then the other. Grant's side of the bed was empty.

His pillow was faintly indented. The covers slightly rumpled. But no broody CEO in sight.

Bathroom?

Nope. The door was cracked open, dark. The soft flicker of a battery-powered candle glowed in the corner.

I sat up, heart doing that weird stutter-step it saved for moments when spiraling was imminent. He probably just needed air. Or space. Or a moment to regret this whole situation in silence.

Still...

I grabbed a candle and padded into the living room.

There he was—Grant, sitting on the couch, elbows on his knees, head bowed like the weight of something he hadn't figured out yet was sitting right there with him. Candlelight carved shadows across his face, sharp and unreadable.

He hadn't heard me.

Which meant I had five seconds to either turn around or admit I already missed him beside me.

"You okay?" I asked, voice softer than I meant it to be.

His head lifted slowly, eyes finding mine—and something in my chest stuttered again.

It wasn't just the look.

It was the heat behind it.

Like he'd been thinking about me. Still was.

Suddenly, I was acutely aware I was wearing nothing but an oversized sleep shirt, barefoot, holding a flickering candle like I was auditioning for a gothic romance reboot.

"Couldn't sleep?" I asked.

He didn't answer right away. Just kept looking at me like I'd short-circuited something vital.

"Not really," he said finally, voice rough.

"Yeah," I said, stepping closer. "Me either."

The air shifted—soft and electric.

Something was happening.

"I didn't mean to wake you," he added.

"You didn't," I lied.

I sat at the other end of the couch. Close, but not touching.

He glanced over. "I don't know what to do with this."

"This?"

"You," he said. "This. Us. Whatever the hell this is."

I froze.

"You're chaos," he continued. "And I don't mean that as an insult."

I arched a brow. "Flattering start."

"You're loud. Bright. Unpredictable. You narrate everything. You argue with produce. You fill a room and don't apologize for it."

"Sounds exhausting," I said.

"It is," he agreed. "And yet I can't stop thinking about you."

My heart caught.

"I came here to clear my head. Not to—" His gaze dropped to my mouth. "Not to want someone."

Oh.

"You're everything I'm not—chaotic where I'm controlled, fire where I'm logic. And somehow, instead of pushing me away, it's what's pulling me in."

The silence pulsed between us.

"There's no algorithm for this," he said. "No logic. But since the second I saw you spinning in the kitchen like a hurricane, it hasn't stopped."

I swallowed. "You're trying to logic your way out of liking me."

"I'm trying to understand it," he said hoarsely. "Because I don't jump without a plan."

I leaned in, just enough to almost touch. "Maybe this doesn't need a plan. Maybe it just is."

He didn't move.

So I did.

Close enough to see the candlelight flicker in his eyes. "For the record," I whispered, "I'm not asking for answers. Just honesty. And maybe a little bravery."

He stared at me like I'd rewritten his code in real time.

"I don't fall fast," he said. "But I dreamt about you just now."

I blinked. "Dreamt?"

He nodded. "You were dancing in the kitchen. Wearing my shirt."

My breath caught.

"Laughing like you always do. Like you've never been afraid."

And just like that, the floor tilted.

Maybe because I felt it too—the gravity shift. The impossibility of what was happening.

So I said quietly:

"Maybe the universe isn't trying to make sense. Maybe it's trying to wake you up."

His gaze dropped to my lips.

"Do you really believe that?" he asked.

"I don't know," I said with a smile. "But I really want to. And I'm kind of hoping you'll stop overthinking long enough to find out."

GRANT

I couldn't think. And I couldn't *not* think. She was too close, too bright—and I wanted her.

"I want you," I said, voice rough.

She leaned back slightly, surprise flashing across her face before a wicked smile took over. "Really?" she whispered. "Because that's exactly what I was hoping for."

That was all it took.

I moved without thinking, closing the space between us in a heartbeat. Her mouth found mine—sharp, sweet, hungry. Her hands slid into my hair like they belonged there. Mine landed on her waist, pulling her into my lap. She settled easily, like this had always been the plan.

I kissed her again, deeper, harder, and she gasped against me.

"Grant," she breathed, wide-eyed, breathless, alive in a way that made my chest ache.

And then—because of course—it was Mia. She laughed. That brilliant, uncontainable laugh that cracked open something in me.

I kissed her again to keep from saying something I'd regret. Or maybe something I wouldn't.

I hadn't known how much I wanted her until she was pressed against me, straddling my lap, her body melting into mine like we'd done this a hundred times.

It was reckless. It was real.

And I didn't care.

Mia Wilder had turned my world upside down in a matter of hours, and I wasn't pretending anymore.

Her mouth on mine was fire and mischief. She shifted in my lap, and a low sound escaped me—half groan, half plea.

She pulled back just enough to smirk. "For a broody CEO, you're surprisingly good at team-building."

I almost laughed. Almost.

"This is insane," she said, eyes dancing.

"Completely."

"I'm not usually this easy."

"Neither am I."

And just like that, she moved again—slow, purposeful—and any thought of restraint vanished.

"Keep doing that," I said, breath catching. "And we're not making it to the bed."

She didn't stop.

Her hands slid up my chest, mouth hot on mine, body pressed close enough to make thought impossible. She broke the kiss to reach for the hem of her oversized shirt.

"Too fast?" she asked softly.

Then the shirt was gone—and so was my sanity.

I swore under my breath. "Not fast enough."

She laughed, low and wicked, and leaned back in. My hands roamed her skin, committing every inch to memory. Her waist, her back, her hips—soft, warm, perfect.

She kissed me again—wild and sweet and unfiltered.

And then she slid off my lap and onto the floor, kneeling between my knees.

My breath caught hard.

She looked up at me, candlelight flickering in her eyes, her hands sliding slowly up my thighs like she already knew what she was doing to me. Or maybe she just liked watching me fall apart.

"Mia," I said—rough, low, already gone.

She hooked her fingers into the waistband of my shorts and tugged.

I sucked in a breath as she wrapped one hand around me, squeezing lightly. Heat shot through me like a live wire. Like nothing I'd felt before.

I was gone.

Completely lost in the way she touched me, the way she looked at me like I was something to devour. Like I'd been hers for far longer than one chaotic night.

She lowered her mouth, and my whole world went white. Hot. Real.

Her mouth—God, her mouth was warm and wet, and I might've actually blacked out for a second.

The first stroke was slow and deliberate. My head fell back, and I swore. Loudly.

"Jesus," I hissed, pure sensation hitting me like a tidal wave.

Her tongue, her lips, the slow drag of heat—it was too much. It wasn't enough. It was everything.

My hands tangled in her hair, holding on like I might come apart otherwise.

She set a pace that unraveled me, each stroke and glide sending pleasure sparking through nerves I didn't know I had. My pulse pounded in time with every move—urgent, wild, and entirely out of control.

She hollowed her cheeks, and my hips bucked.

"Mia," I groaned, voice ragged and raw. "God."

I was breaking, undone in the best possible way. Completely, utterly wrecked.

And then she went deeper—took more—and the bottom dropped out of my world.

I let out a sharp sound, my body tensing hard as release tore through me fast and fierce. My vision blurred. My grip tightened in her hair as waves of heat rolled through every inch of skin and bone, long and unrelenting.

For a second, I forgot how to breathe.

Then she eased up slowly, her touch gentle and reverent as I returned to myself. As my pulse stopped, trying to set new speed records. As my mind caught up with my body, I realized what had just happened. Holy shit.

I let out a shaky breath.

Everything felt unsteady in the best possible way.

Mia leaned back on her heels, eyes bright and wicked in the candlelight. She looked like chaos and desire and victory. Like she knew exactly what she'd done.

Like she loved every second.

A slow smile curved her mouth as she knelt there.

I reached for her.

She didn't resist—just let me pull her back into my lap, soft and satisfied and somehow even more dangerous than before.

My hands slid up her back, hungry for more.

"Your turn," I murmured against her throat.

Chapter Seven

MIA

GRANT EASED ME TO the edge of the couch and knelt between my legs.

Then his mouth closed over my nipple—kissing, teasing, then grazing it with his teeth—and I shattered.

"Grant," I gasped, arching into him.

He made a low sound that vibrated through me, then shifted to the other breast, tongue stroking in slow, maddening circles until I was a mess beneath him.

His mouth moved lower, trailing heat down my stomach until he reached the waistband of my thong. His breath hit my skin—and I was already gone.

He glanced up, eyes dark with intent, then kissed me through the lace.

My hips bucked. My pulse spiked. The friction was electric.

I cried out—raw, wild, completely undone—and he didn't stop. He just deepened the pressure, licking through the fabric with relentless, knowing precision.

By the time I realized the thong was gone, his mouth was back—bare, direct, devastating.

White-hot urgency built fast—too fast—but I couldn't stop it. Couldn't slow down. Couldn't do anything but gasp his name and hope I survived this intact.

"Grant," I panted as his tongue circled and teased, "Oh my God."

I was a live wire. A frayed end. A spark about to ignite.

And then he slid two fingers inside me, and I exploded.

The world went bright, then dark, then bright again as pleasure crashed over me in a dizzying wave. I heard myself moan, loud and long and completely undone.

His mouth didn't stop—he kept stroking as I shattered around him, pulling every last bit of sensation from my body.

It was too much. It was nowhere near enough.

I was still trembling when he finally eased up, both of us breathing hard in the candlelit dark.

"Wow." The word came out on a breathless laugh. "For a broody CEO, you really don't cut corners."

He grinned against my thigh. "I pride myself on being thorough."

I pulled him up to me, desperate for more contact, for another taste of the man who'd just destroyed me in the best possible way.

His mouth covered mine—hot and demanding—and I could taste myself on his lips. It sent another jolt through me.

He kissed me like he was starving, rolling us so I was straddling him again, skin against skin.

I broke the kiss, breathless. "Is this too much? I mean—do you need a minute? Or can we—?"

Grant flipped us, pinning me beneath him, already hard against my thigh.

"Trust me," he said roughly, "I'm ready."

I wrapped my legs around him—but he froze.

"What?" I asked.

He blinked. "Condoms. I didn't bring any."

I groaned. "Seriously?"

"I wasn't planning for this."

"Neither was I." I sat up, brushing hair out of my face. "You were not part of my relaxation itinerary."

He muttered something under his breath, glancing toward the bedroom. "Maybe the resort included... essentials."

"Emergency romance supplies?" I was already up, candle in hand. "Let's find out."

I grabbed the candle and sprinted to the bedroom, flinging open drawers like a prize was at the bottom of each.

"Bingo!" I yelled, holding up a foil packet. Then two. "We're officially saved!"

Grant sat up, looking equal parts turned on and relieved.

I shut the door behind me, climbed into his lap, and handed him one.

He opened it with his teeth—of course—and rolled it on with practiced focus that nearly broke me all over again.

"I want you," he said, voice low as he lifted me.

One smooth thrust and he was inside me—hot, thick, perfect.

"Grant!" I gasped, rocking against him, pulse spiking as the pressure built with each slow, perfect stroke.

His hands gripped my hips, guiding me and setting a rhythm that made it clear neither of us would last long. Desperate sounds escaped my mouth with every move—his name, my breath—a wild symphony in the quiet.

"God," he groaned, eyes dark as they watched me ride him. "Mia."

Hearing my name on his lips did it—I shattered again, harder than before, breaking apart around him with a cry.

He followed fast—a low, deep sound tearing from his throat as he drove into me one last time. His release hit hard enough that I could feel it even through the condom, an electric pulse through my core.

We stayed tangled together, chests heaving, skin slick, hearts pounding like they were racing each other.

Neither of us moved.

GRANT

We stayed like that—tangled, silent, real. The storm still howled outside, but for the first time, it didn't matter.

Eventually, we moved. Just long enough to clean up, crawl into bed, and remember how to breathe.

Mia curled into me, her hair wild against my chest, the blanket pulled over us like a truce with the world. I traced the curve of her shoulder, breathing in the warm, unmistakable scent of us.

"Wow," she murmured on a soft exhale. "The universe really knows how to crash a vacation."

"Not complaining," I said into her hair.

She hummed. "So... fate? Or just two stranded people with very good timing?"

I didn't answer right away. Her skin was warm, her breath a whisper against my neck.

"I think it doesn't matter what it's called," I said quietly.

She shifted, lifting her face just enough to meet my gaze.

"We're here," I added. "And that's enough."

She smiled.

So I kissed her—slow, deep, unhurried. Like we had all night. Like there was no world outside this room.

But my body had other ideas.

It surged back to life with a speed that surprised even me, pulling her closer like it couldn't bear to let her go.

Mia laughed softly against my mouth. "Do you ever run out of batteries?"

I pulled back just enough to meet her eyes. "You're one to talk."

Then I flipped her onto her stomach with one smooth motion.

She was quick to catch on, her hips lifting, back arching as I slid behind her.

The view was incredible. She was incredible. I quickly slipped on another condom and traced a line down her spine, my pulse racing to keep up with the rest of me.

Mia made a low, impatient, and urgent sound, so I gave us exactly what we wanted.

One deep thrust and I was inside her again—deep and breathless and sinking into the kind of heat that made every single thought disappear except this one: How had I survived this long without her?

She let out a sharp moan, pushing back against me with a rhythm that was pure instinct. Pure need. Her hand tangled in the sheets. Her hair tumbled over one bare shoulder. Her skin was gold against the candlelight, her body warm and alive beneath mine.

Jesus Christ.

I picked up the pace, each thrust taking us closer to the edge. Mia's breaths turned ragged—the kind of gasps that would ruin me if they hadn't already.

"Grant," she panted, voice barely there but everything I needed to hear.

I shifted slightly, changing the angle until she cried out and dropped her head against the pillow. Until nothing else mattered except our breath and bodies and how goddamn good this felt.

I wanted this forever. Wanted her forever.

The thought hit hard—fast enough to have me tensing as release slammed through, fast enough to have me clenching my jaw as she shattered again beneath me, a low groan escaping my throat as I followed right behind her with a final thrust.

We collapsed forward together, her hair spilling across my chest, both of us breathing hard and not moving for a long time.

We stayed like that—breathless and tangled with the storm, her heartbeat under my hand and mine under hers. I should have been exhausted. Or worried. Or making a mental list of all the ways this would explode in my face when the real world caught up.

But somehow, I wasn't.

Somehow, I didn't care.

There'd be time for questions later. For logic, labels, and all the things we were supposed to talk about but hadn't yet.

But not tonight.

Tonight, I was going to let this be what it was. Real. Unexpected. Exactly where I wanted to be.

I pulled her closer.

She made a soft sound in her sleep, curling into me like she already knew how this story ended.

And for once, I wasn't in a rush to find out.

So I closed my eyes.

And let myself rest.

Chapter Eight

MIA

I WOKE UP TO gray skies and Grant's hand on my ass.

To be fair—it was a very nice hand. And clearly confident in its new home, resting warm and solid against bare skin like it had no intention of relocating.

I didn't hate it.

Stretching slightly, I felt the delicious ache of muscles thoroughly used in... every way possible. The blanket shifted, but Grant didn't stir—just made a low, sleepy sound that went straight to my core and tightened his grip.

So that's how it was going to be.

I burrowed closer, a smile tugging at my lips. The storm had eased—not gone, but no longer threatening to launch us into the ocean. Which, considering the total lack of clothing, would've made for an awkward evacuation.

And what a night.

The memory made me grin. Still vivid, still electric. My body buzzed in all the best ways, my heart doing this odd little tap dance, and my brain? Absolutely no use to me.

I shifted to look at him.

Rumpled hair, slack jaw, faintest smile like the night had followed him into his dreams. He looked peaceful. Vulnerable. Like maybe he'd stay here forever if no one reminded him of the real world.

A reckless little voice whispered that maybe he could stay right here instead.

I pressed a soft kiss to his chest—no expectations, just... thanks. Just warmth.

He stirred, muttered something incoherent, then blinked awake—slow and disoriented but still, unfairly, stupidly attractive.

"Hey there, sleepy CEO," I teased. "We survived. The storm. The night. Each other. Barely."

His arm tightened around me, but his smile didn't quite reach his eyes. "Morning."

"Well," I said lightly, "I can officially cross 'unexpected island fling' off my bucket list."

It was a joke. A harmless deflection. Something breezy to ease the swirl of too many feelings I wasn't ready to name.

But something shifted in Grant.

Not big. Not obvious. Just enough to register like a flicker in the light.

He didn't tense. Didn't flinch.

He just... went still.

His arm, once wrapped around me, loosened. His hand drifted from my skin like he'd suddenly remembered where we were.

When he finally spoke, his voice was quiet. Neutral.

"Right. Guess that's one way to look at it."

And just like that, the warmth cracked.

Barely. But enough.

Maybe it was nothing. Maybe he was tired. Processing. Already mentally triaging his inbox. But I felt the space open up between us—small but unmistakable.

I tried again.

"Technically, I should probably also cross off 'survive a tropical storm,' but that feels less impressive."

He made a noncommittal sound. Not a laugh. Not even close.

I glanced over.

He was sitting up now, the sheet around his waist, back turned to me as he reached for a glass of water. Every movement was calm. Measured. Polite.

Like he was rehearsing distance.

"I'm gonna take a quick shower," he said without turn-ing.

The words were casual. But the door closing behind him felt like a curtain dropping.

I stayed in bed, staring at the ceiling, blanket tucked around me like armor.

Maybe I was imagining things. Maybe it wasn't weird. Maybe I was overthinking it.

But the truth sat heavy in my chest, unwelcome and unshakable.

It mattered.

And that scared me more than I wanted to admit.

GRANT

The water was too hot.

Or maybe I was trying to scald the confusion off my skin.

I braced my hands against the tile, let the spray pound down my back, and tried to believe it would help. It didn't.

All I could think about was Mia.

The way she smiled when she thought I was asleep. The way she kissed my chest like it was second nature. The way her voice caught when she said "unexpected island fling," like she needed me to laugh before she found out it wasn't funny.

She wasn't wrong. On paper, that's exactly what this was. Two strangers. A storm. A shared bungalow and a night neither of us had planned.

But it didn't *feel* like that.

It felt like something had shifted. Something real. Something I couldn't quantify or control.

And I didn't know what to do with it.

Because I don't do chaos. I don't do off-plan.

But Mia? She *was* chaos. Wild, brilliant, impossible to ignore.

And here I was—standing in the middle of it, soaked and stunned, already wondering what I'd do when it ended. When she left.

Because last night didn't feel temporary.

It felt like the start of something I didn't understand.

And that terrified me.

Because I didn't know if it was real to her, too—or if I was just a vacation story.

A knock at the door.

Soft. Hesitant.

Then: "Grant?"

I froze. Steam clung to my skin, thick and suffocating.

I wasn't ready. Not for her. Not for this.

But Mia had never waited for *ready*.

"I'm coming in," she said—and a beat later, the door opened just enough for her to slip inside.

"Okay," she started, arms crossed, eyes searching. "Here's the deal. I don't know what last night meant to you. I'm not trying to be dramatic, or slap labels on feelings that haven't even figured out their names yet."

She paused—breathed like she had to steady herself.

"But I know what it meant to me. And I need to know if I'm the only one who felt it."

The air changed.

"I didn't plan this," she went on, softer now. "I didn't come here looking for anyone. Especially not someone like you. But then you showed up—with your stormy eyes and your spreadsheets and that ridiculous jawline—"

I made a choked sound. She ignored it.

"I like you, Grant," she said. "In a way that's terrifying and weirdly honest. And maybe this was just a fling for you. Maybe you're already halfway out the mental door. But I need to know. Was it real? Or just... the storm?"

My chest was tight. My mind was chaos.

And still—I reached for her.

No logic. No hesitation. Just instinct.

I stepped out of the spray, water streaming down my body, and took her hand. She didn't flinch. Just looked up at me like she was bracing for the worst.

Instead, I pulled her forward—closer—until the water hit her too. Her breath caught.

"Mia," I said, my voice rough and low, "it's real."

Her eyes searched mine.

"I don't know what to do with it. I didn't expect this. I didn't want this. But it's real. You're in my head. You're under my skin. And I don't want it to stop."

Water slid down her face. Her lashes. Her lips.

She looked like a painting come to life. Too vivid. Too much.

Exactly what I needed.

"I came here to shut the world out," I whispered, my forehead resting against hers. "But you showed up. And now I don't want to go back to before."

She swallowed. "So it wasn't just the storm?"

I shook my head. "It was you."

Then I kissed her.

Slow. Certain. Like I already knew I'd never get enough.

She kissed me back with that same urgency, her hands in my hair, her body pressing close. I backed her against the tile, the heat between us sharper than the spray.

She gasped, then laughed—a low sound that wrecked me in the best way.

"Grant," she whispered.

I lifted her easily, her legs wrapping around me like they belonged there.

And then I was inside her—deep and sure and exactly where I wanted to be.

The heat was instant. The rhythm, instinct.

Her moans echoed in the steam as I moved, her fingers clutching my shoulders, her body arching to meet every thrust.

"God," she panted, head falling back against the wall, "this—"

I kissed her again, swallowing the rest of her words. Her cries. Her breath.

We didn't stop.

Didn't slow.

It was fast and hot and overwhelming—like something had been unleashed between us. A promise. A reckoning.

And when we came—together, hard—it felt like gravity broke and rebuilt itself around us.

We held on like we meant it.

And this time, I didn't wonder if she'd walk away.

I just held her tighter.

Because for the first time in longer than I could remember—I didn't want to be anywhere else.

Chapter Nine

GRANT

WHEN WE FINALLY STUMBLED out of the shower, soaked, unsteady, and more tangled than ever, I dried off with a towel too big for one person but just right for two. Mia laughed into the fabric, bright and breathless, like maybe everything would be fine—as long as we stayed exactly where we were.

"Wow," she said when we finally came up for air. "That was... thorough."

"Fast learner," I said with a grin that felt way too easy.

And for a moment, it was just that—easy.

No second thoughts. No exit strategies. Just two people who'd found something unexpected in the middle of a storm and decided not to let it go.

Then the lights flickered.

Once. Twice.

And then—on.

A low whir buzzed through the walls as power surged back into the bungalow. The fridge kicked on. A few forgotten lamps blinked back to life. And from somewhere behind me, Mia made a noise that could only be described as a *victorious squeak*.

"I have never loved electricity more," she said, holding the towel like a cape and marching triumphantly toward the bed.

I didn't even make it two steps after her before the phone rang.

We both froze.

Mia turned slowly, eyes wide. "If that's your secret bungalow girlfriend calling, now would be the time to mention it."

I rolled my eyes and turned to the landline. "This is Grant Ashford," I said as I picked up the phone. Then, I hit the speaker button and set the phone down so Mia could hear.

A pause. Then a voice—brisk, polite, and clearly running on hotel-concern autopilot—came through the speaker.

"Mr. Ashford, good morning. This is Lena from the front desk. We're calling to check in with all guests after the outage. Is everything alright at your location?"

"We're fine," I said, glancing at Mia, who was now dramatically draped across the bed like a Roman empress in a towel. "No issues."

"I'm delighted to hear that," Lena said, a note of relief in her voice. "While reviewing the registry this morning, we discovered that your bungalow was accidentally double-booked just before the storm. We sincerely apologize for the oversight. We've prepared a second bungalow and are ready to move one of you there immediately—of course, both vacations will be fully comped."

I glanced at Mia.

She arched a brow, then—without breaking eye contact—let her towel slip just enough off one shoulder to hint at all the reasons we didn't need two bungalows.

My throat went dry.

"Actually," I said quickly, turning back to the phone with the poise of a man barely hanging onto his sanity, "that won't be necessary. We're perfectly comfortable."

Mia bit her lip and gave me an innocent look that was anything but.

"Very well," the woman on the line said, sounding slightly confused. "If you change your mind at any point, please don't hesitate to—"

"Thanks, will do," I said, cutting her off with practiced corporate efficiency. "Have a great day."

Then I hung up.

MIA

Grant was still watching me. Barely holding it together. Which, honestly? Fair.

I adjusted my towel like it was a designer gown, struck a regal pose on the bed, and sweetly said, "Were you saying something about separate accommodations?"

He narrowed his eyes. "You're evil."

I beamed. "I know."

He sat down on the edge of the bed, quiet like the air had shifted.

"So," he said.

"So?" I echoed one brow lifting.

He let out a slow breath. "Now what?"

My stomach did a little flip.

"Like, existentially?" I asked. "Or are we talking about breakfast?"

He gave me a look. The kind that said *don't deflect this, Mia*.

I sobered. Just a little. "You mean now that the storm is over?"

He nodded.

I looked at him, really looked at him. Rumpled hair. That impossible jawline. The softest trace of uncertainty in eyes that had felt like home last night.

"Do you want there to be a 'now what'?" I asked.

His eyes didn't leave mine. "Yes."

My breath caught.

"I don't know what this is," he said. "I don't know what it turns into. But I know it doesn't feel over."

A smile tugged at the corner of my mouth. "Good. Because if you'd said 'thanks for the memories,' I was fully prepared to weaponize this towel."

He laughed—quiet and low like it slipped past his defenses. "Please don't. I'm not equipped for that kind of warfare."

I leaned in heart thudding. "Then let's figure it out."

He didn't answer right away. Just looked at me like he wasn't sure how this happened—how *we* happened. And honestly? I didn't know either. But I knew what I wanted.

So when he reached across the bed and took my hand, I let him.

"I want more than one storm," he said, voice rough.

My breath hitched.

And in that moment, something clicked into place. Not perfectly. Not neatly. But enough.

He was logic. I was chaos. But maybe—just maybe—we were figuring it out anyway.

Epilogue

MIA

Six months later...

The storm rolled in like déjà vu.

Thunder, low and steady. Rain streaked down the windows in frantic bursts. The city outside blurred into light and wet pavement—but in here, wrapped in Grant's arms, skin still warm from the shower and his breath steady against my neck, it felt like the calmest place in the world.

Lightning cracked across the sky, lighting up the room for one bright, heart-stopping beat.

I flinched.

He didn't.

He just tightened his hold—like he remembered exactly how to anchor me when the world got loud.

"I used to hate storms," I murmured, fingers tracing idle shapes across his chest. "They made me feel... unmoored. Like everything could fall apart at once. But now?"

I looked up at him, my heartbeat tapping wild against my ribs.

"Now I kinda like them. Maybe because I finally have something solid to hold on to."

Grant didn't smile. Didn't tease.

He just looked at me—like I'd said something far more profound than I meant it to be.

"I love you," he said quietly.

Like it wasn't a confession.

Like it was a fact.

Like gravity.

I blinked at him. "You can't just say that when I'm not emotionally braced for it."

He tilted his head slightly, lips twitching at the corners. "Seemed like the right time."

My throat went tight.

And for a second, I did what I always did—opened my mouth, ready to toss back something sarcastic. Deflect with humor. Keep it light.

But nothing came out.

Because I felt it too.

All of it. Crashing through me with the same reckless certainty that brought me to his bed in the middle of a tropical storm and never quite let me go.

"I love you," I whispered, eyes stinging. "God help me, I really do."

He smiled then—small, quiet, steady—and pulled me in like it was the easiest thing in the world.

Outside, the storm raged on.

But inside?

We were finally home.

***

Dear Reader,

Thank you so much for reading *Unraveling Mr. Ashford*! I hope you had as much fun diving into Mia and Grant's wild, storm-swept romance as I did writing it—every chaotic moment, steamy kiss, and emotionally loaded banter.

This story was my love letter to opposites attracting in the best (and most inconvenient) way: a fiercely creative, caffeine-fueled chaos goddess accidentally marooned with a grumpy, logic-driven tech billionaire who just wanted silence. Spoiler alert: he got Mia instead—and absolutely no peace and quiet.

Writing Mia was pure joy—she's all sparkle, sass, and unfiltered heart—and watching her unravel Grant's carefully controlled world? *Chef's kiss.* And Grant? Underneath the brooding brilliance? A total goner the second she rearranged that fruit bowl.

If their story made you laugh, swoon, or feel a little less alone in your own stormy moments, I'd be so grateful if you left a review. Just a few words go a long way in helping other readers find this series. You can review the book on Amazon.

Thank you again for spending time with these two—your support means the world.

Until next time—with love (and probably a very strong coffee),

Hana York

***

Loved *Unraveling Mr. Ashford*? Don't miss the rest of the *Don't Fall for the Billionaire* series! Each book is packed with swoon-worthy heroes, strong heroines, and plenty of sparks. If you haven't read them yet, here's what you're missing:

Book One: *Hating Mr. Wentworth*

They're supposed to be enemies—so why does arguing feel like foreplay?

Liz Bentley built her career on grit, caffeine, and a zero-tolerance policy for entitled men—especially not the newly appointed CEO with a famous last name and a face straight off a magazine cover. Brett Wentworth might be rich, polished, and maddeningly smug, but Liz knows his type: privilege, power, and betrayal wrapped in a designer suit.

Brett didn't ask to inherit the mess his father made of Bright Spark. But the moment Liz storms into his boardroom—all fire, wit, and defiance—he knows two things: she's the sharpest mind in the company... and the one woman he shouldn't want.

Their arguments are electric. Their chemistry, impossible to ignore. And one dangerously hot encounter changes everything.

Now Brett has one shot to prove he's nothing like the men who came before—and everything Liz never saw coming.

Enemies on paper. Fireworks in person. A hot, hilarious romance that's one HR violation away from disaster—or the most delicious kind of downfall.

Hating Mr. Wentworth **is available on Amazon.**

Book Two: *Tempting Dr. Dawson*

A sizzling, laugh-out-loud billionaire romcom about mistaken identity, forbidden chemistry, and the hidden moment that might just lead to love.

Travel writer Piper Winslow is in paradise—but she's not here to relax. Her assignment? Review Coral Bay Resort and keep things strictly professional. But the guy in the Hawaiian shirt who offers her a "real" tour of the property? He's messing with her objectivity—and tempting her to break all her rules.

Logan Dawson didn't mean to lie. When Piper mistakes him for a charming staff member instead of the CEO of the luxury resort she's reviewing, he doesn't correct her. For once, someone sees him, not his title. And walking away from that? Not so easy.

What starts as playful banter turns into an afternoon of unforgettable heat in a hidden grotto. But when the truth comes out, so does the fallout. Now Logan has to prove that the man she fell for is the real him—and that what sparked between them wasn't just a vacation fling.

Tempting Mr. Dawson is a steamy billionaire romcom with sharp banter, tropical heat, mistaken identities, and a CEO who'll risk everything to win back the woman who saw through him.

Tempting Mr. Dawson **is available on Amazon.**

Hana York Books

Hearts on Duty Series

Sparks of Temptation

Love's Anchor

On Call for You

Investigating Desire

Falling for the Rescue

A Heart Worth Mending

***

Don't Fall for the Billionaire Series

Hating Mr. Wentworth

Tempting Mr. Dawson

Unraveling Mr. Ashford

For a full list of titles, please visit Hana York's website

www.HanaYork.com

About the Author

Hana York writes fast-paced, heart-pounding contemporary romance packed with irresistible heroes, strong heroines, laugh-out-loud banter, and just the right amount of spice to keep things sizzling. Her books are for readers who love grumpy men falling hard, fierce women who don't need saving, and the kind of chemistry that sparks off the page.

When she's not crafting stories full of love, tension, and toe-curling moments, you'll find her daydreaming about small-town charm, plotting ridiculous meet-cutes, and consuming an unhealthy amount of coffee. She believes in happily-ever-afters, overprotective heroes who don't stand a chance against their heroines, and that every great love story should come with a side of sass.

If you love forced proximity, off-limits attraction, sizzling tension, and romance that makes your heart race, welcome to the world of Hana York!

Follow Hana York for new releases, exclusive content, and behind-the-scenes fun! www.HanaYork.com

Find all her books here: https://www.amazon.com/author/hanayork

Follow her on Instagram: https://www.instagram.com/hanayorkromance/

Follow her on Facebook: https://www.facebook.com/hanayorkromance/

Follow her on Good Reads: https://www.goodreads.com/author/show/54826946.Hana_York

Join her mailing list here: https://www.hanayork.com/subscribe